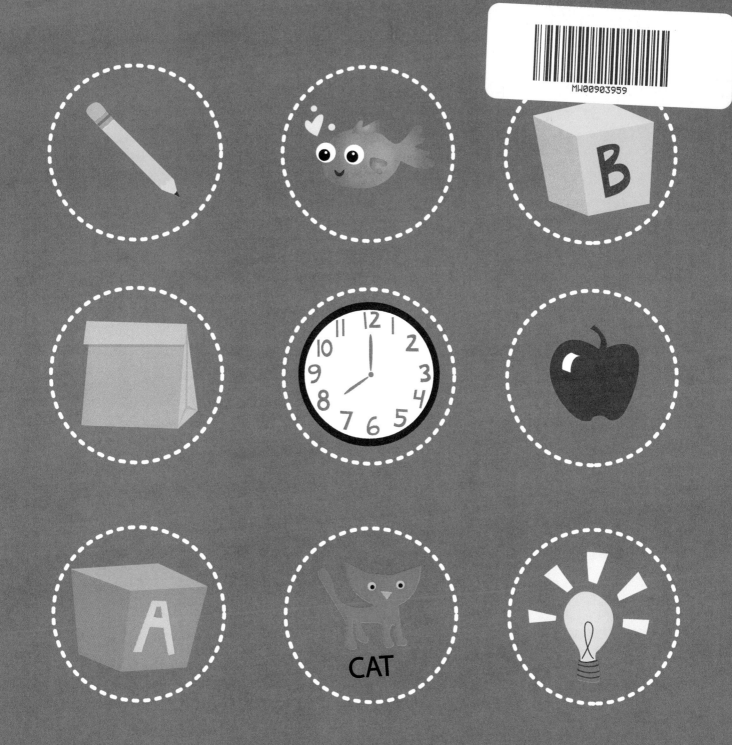

CAT

First Edition
Library Binding ISBN: 9781532409349
Paperback ISBN: 978-1-5324-0904-2
eISBN: 978-1-5324-0903-5
Published in the United States by Xist Publishing
www.xistpublishing.com
PO Box 61593 Irvine, CA 92602

Little Hoo
Goes to School

Brenda Ponnay

Good morning, Little Hoo!

It's time to get ready
for your first day of school!

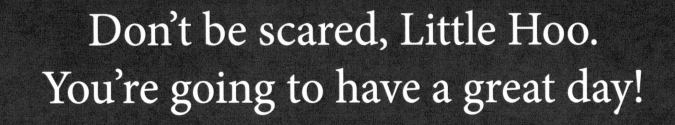

Don't be scared, Little Hoo.
You're going to have a great day!

Are you scared
you're going to miss
Mama Hoo?

Don't worry, Little Hoo.
You are probably going to have
so much fun you won't have time
to even miss Mama Hoo!

Are you scared
you won't
like your teacher?

Are you worried that learning new things will be too hard?

Don't worry, Little Hoo.
Learning new things can be fun!

Are you worried you are going
to miss your stuffed owl
at home?

Don't worry, Little Hoo, your stuffed owl will be waiting for you when you get home.

And you will probably make new
friends to keep you company!

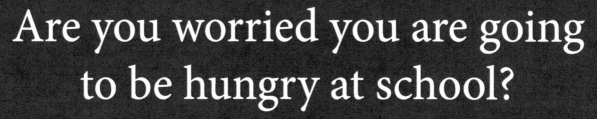

Are you worried you are going to be hungry at school?

Don't worry Little Hoo,
Mama Hoo will pack you
a special lunch!

See, Little Hoo,
everything is going to be fine.
Let's go to school!

You are going to have a great day!